# PREFACE

In the ancient wisdom of Sanatana Dharma, sound is not merely vibration—it is creation, transformation, and transcendence. From the primordial syllable Om to the powerful invocations of the Vedas, mantras have always held a sacred place in Hindu spiritual practice. They are more than chants; they are the bridge between the seeker and the divine, guiding one inward toward self-realization and outward toward universal harmony.

Mantra Sādhana is a humble compilation of sacred Hindu mantras, curated with deep reverence and spiritual intent. Each mantra in this collection carries the vibration of centuries of devotion, whispered in temples, chanted in homes, and meditated upon in solitude by sages and seekers alike. Whether it is a mantra for peace, strength, healing, prosperity, or spiritual awakening, this book seeks to serve as a trusted companion for all who walk the path of devotion (bhakti), discipline (sādhana), and inner transformation.

# PREFACE

As the Founder and Director of Sthiti Yoga, my journey through yoga has been one of healing, discovery, and deep connection with the source. This compilation arises from a personal longing to make these timeless chants accessible and available to all who wish to imbibe their grace—be it in daily practice, rituals, or meditation.

May this book be a doorway to stillness, strength, and spiritual awakening. May every mantra spoken from your lips bloom into divine experience. And may your sādhana be blessed with sincerity, steadiness, and light.

# ABOUT STHITI YOGA

Sthiti Yoga was born out of a vision to bring balance, healing, and spiritual alignment into people's lives through the timeless science of yoga. Founded by Sangeetha Ravindran, a dedicated yogic healer with an M.Sc in Yoga and a profound understanding of its therapeutic and transformative powers, Sthiti Yoga is a space where tradition meets intention, and movement meets stillness.

The Sanskrit word "Sthiti" means condition, state, position, or situation - qualities that are not only essential in asana but are the very foundation of a meaningful life.

At its heart, Sthiti Yoga is more than a studio—it is a spiritual sanctuary, a learning space, and a healing community.

Whether you are beginning your journey or deepening an existing practice, Sthiti Yoga welcomes you with authenticity, compassion, and the unwavering aim to guide you inward—where true stillness and strength reside.

# CONTENT

# CONTENT

# mantra

a word or sound of vibrational power best recited repeatedly to aid in cultivating focus, insight, & connection.

01

# MANTRA

## Meaning, History and Importance

Mantra is the fifth yoga described in the Yoga Upanishads. The word mantra is generally translated as sound vibration. The literal meaning of mantra is 'the force that liberates the mind from bondage', or Mananat trayate iti mantrah - Mantra is that which frees the mind from the shackles by which it is bound.

Another definition is given in the Hatharatnavali (1:19): The letter 'man' is for manas, the mind, and the letter 'tra' is said to be for prana. By connecting manas and prana the yoga is called mantra yoga. Mantra yoga is an ancient science of personal transformation. It uses sound energy in the form of vibration which has a beneficial, harmonizing influence on the mind and the mental activity. The power of mantra lies not in the words, or their meaning but in the specific vibrations created when the mantra is chanted.

Regular practice of mantra frees the mind of mental conditions and limitations that are the cause of unhappiness, worry, trouble, greed, fear and anger. Sustained practice of mantra brings calmness, peace and serenity to the restless mind.

Therefore, the practice of mantra is a scientific process and does not relate to religious concepts or names of any god or deity. There need not be any conflict between the religion you follow and your mantra.

# TYPES OF MANTRA CHANTING

### <u>Vaikhari Japa (Loud Chanting):</u>
This is the most basic form, where the mantra is chanted aloud. It's often considered the starting point for mantra practice.

### <u>Upamsu Japa (Whispered or Low Chanting):</u>
The mantra is repeated softly, with the tongue and lips moving. It's an intermediate level of chanting.

### <u>Manasika Japa (Mental Chanting):</u>
This involves chanting the mantra mentally, without any physical movement of the mouth or tongue. It's considered an advanced practice.

### <u>Likhita Japa (Writing the Mantra):</u>
This involves repeatedly writing the mantra.

# OM & AUM

In Sanskrit, when the vowels "a" (अ) or "ā" (आ) are followed by "u" (उ) or "ū" (ऊ), they combine to form the vowel "o" (ओ).

$$(अ, आ) + (उ, ऊ) \rightarrow ओ$$

This means that if there is "a" or "ā" followed by "u" or "ū", the combination results in the sound "o"

# SOHAM MANTRA
## Initially 21 Times

Soham or Sohum is a mantra, literally meaning "That (is) I" in Sanskrit, implying "I am that".

Soham mantra meditation involves repeating the mantra while focusing on the breath. Inhale while mentally saying "So" and exhale while saying "Hum". This helps to calm the mind, increase concentration, and cultivate a sense of self-awareness.

*"So" (with the breath in) and "Ham" (with the breath out)*

**Padmasana - Lotus pose or Sukhasana - Easy pose**

# JAPA MEDITATION

Japa meditation is a form of meditation that uses mantras to quiet and focus the mind. It is, also known as mantra meditation, is a practice that involves the repeated recitation of a mantra (a sacred sound, word, or phrase) as a means of meditation and spiritual growth. It's a way to calm the mind, enhance focus, and elevate consciousness. The core of japa is the conscious repetition of the mantra, either vocally or mentally, according to Big Shakti.

# OM NAMAH SHIVAYA
## 108 Times

Om Namah Shivaya" translates to "I bow to Shiva" or "Salutations to Shiva". The mantra is a powerful invocation dedicated to Lord Shiva, a major deity in Hinduism, particularly within the Shaiva tradition.

*Om- The symbol used in every mantra*
*Namah- To give respect*
*Shivay- God Shiva*

# GAYATRI MANTRA

## 11 Times

*Om:* Essence of the ultimate reality.

*Bhur Bhuvah Swah:* Nature of God, showing His existence in different planes – the Earth, the atmosphere, and heaven.

*Tat Savitur Varenyam:* A prayer to the divine Savitur, the Sun God, to enlighten our minds.

*Bhargo Devasya Dhimahi:* Meditating on the divine light, seeking spiritual wisdom.

*Dhiyo Yo Naḥ Prachodayat:* A prayer for guidance, asking the divine to illuminate our intellect.

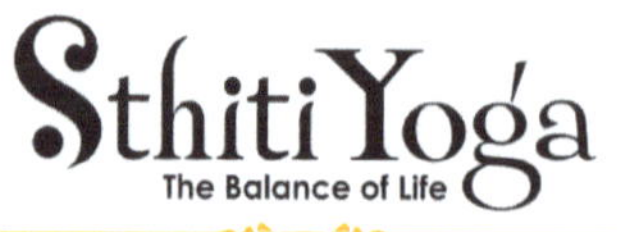

# MRITHUNJAYA MANTRA
## 11 Times

The Mahamrityunjaya Mantra is a verse of the Rigveda. The ṛc is addressed to Tryambaka, "The Three-eyed One", an epithet of Rudra who is identified with Shiva in Shaivism. The verse also recurs in the Yajurveda.

*Aum Tryambakam yajaamahe sugandhim pushtivardhanam |*
*Urvaarukamiva bandhanaan-mrityormuksheeya maamritaat ||*

We worship the three-eyed One, who is fragrant and who nourishes all. Like the fruit falls off from the bondage of the stem, may we be liberated from death, from mortality.

# 32 DURGA NAMES
## 3 Times

*Durga – The reliever of difficulties*

*Durgartishamani – Who puts difficulties at peace*

*Durgapadvinivarini – Dispeller of difficult adversities*

*Durgamachchhedani – Who cuts down difficulty*

*Durgasadhini – The performer of discipline to expel difficulties*

*Durganashini – The destroyer of difficulty*

*Durgatoddharini – Who holds the whip of difficulties*

*Durganihantri – Who sends difficulties to ruin*

*Durgamapaha – Who measures difficulties*

*Durgamagyanada – Who makes difficulties unconscious*

*Durgadaityalokadavanala – Who destroys the world of*
*difficult thoughts*

*Durgama – The mother of difficulties*

*Durgamaloka – The perception of difficulties*

*Durgamatmaswarupini – The intrinsic nature of the soul*
*of difficulties*

*Durgamargaprada – Who searches through the difficulties*

*Durgamavidya – The knowledge of difficulties*

*Durgamashrita – The extrication from difficulties*

# 32 DURGA NAMES
## 3 Times

*Durgamagyanasamsthana – The continued existence of difficulties*

*Durgamadhyanabhasini – Whose meditation remains brilliant when in difficulties*

*Durgamoha – Who deludes difficulties*

*Durgamaga – Who resolves difficulties*

*Durgamarthaswarupini – Who is the intrinsic nature of the object of difficulties*

*Durgamasurasamhantri – The annihilator of the egotism of difficulties*

*Durgamayudhadharini – Bearer of the weapon against difficulties*

*Durgamangi – The refinery of difficulties*

*Durgamata – Who is beyond difficulties*

*Durgamya – This present difficulty*

*Durgameshwari – The empress of difficulties*

*Durgabhima – Who is terrible to difficulties*

*Durgabhama – The lady to difficulties*

*Durgabha – The illuminator of difficulties*

*Durgadarini – Who cuts off difficulties*

# GURU MANTRA

*Guru Brahma, Guru Vishnu,*
*Guru Devo Maheshwaraha,*
*Guru Saakshaat Para Brahma,*
*Tasmai Shri Gurave Namaha*

The Guru is Bramha.
The Guru is Vishnu.
The Guru is Lord Shiva.
The Guru is truly the supreme Brahman.
My salutations (greetings) are to that Guru.
Salutations to the Guru who has made it possible
to realize him.
By whom this entire universe of movable and
immovable objects is pervaded.

# SHANTI MANTRA - I

*Om sahanaavvatu*
*Sah nau bhunaktu*
*Sah veeryan karvaav hai*
*Tejaswi naavadhitamastu maa vidvishaav hai*
*Om shaantih shaantih shaantih*

Om , May He protect us both!
May He enable us to enjoy and work hard in
the pursuit of knowledge!
May we attain brilliance in our study!
May we not quarrel with each other!
Om Peace! Peace! Peace!

13

# SHANTI MANTRA - II

*Om Sarve Bhavantu Sukhinah*
*Sarve Santu Niraamayaah*
*Sarve Bhadraani Pashyantu*
*Maa Kashchid Duhkha Bhaag Bhavet*
*Om Shantih Shantih Shantih*

May all be happy! (sukhinah)
May all be free from disabilities! (niraamayaah)
May all look (pashyantuto the good of others!
May none suffer from sorrow! (duhkha)
Om Peace! Peace! Peace!

# SHANTI MANTRA - III

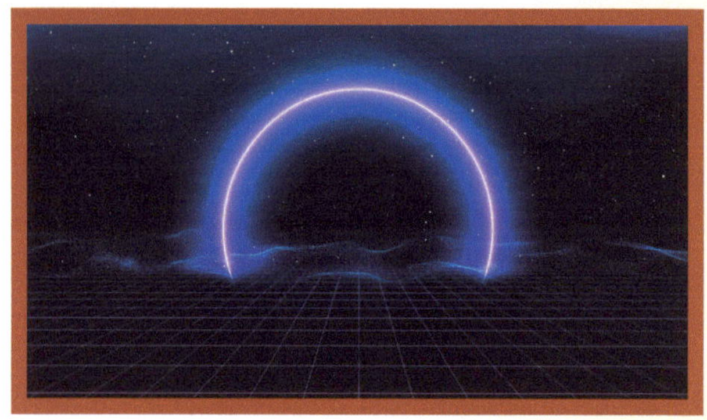

*Om Sarveshaam Svastir-Bhavatu*
*Sarveshaam Shaantir-Bhavatu*
*Sarveshaam Purnnam-Bhavatu*
*Sarveshaam Manggalam-Bhavatu*
*Om Shaantih Shaantih Shaantih*

The mantra "Om Sarvesham svastir Bhavatu" is a powerful Sanskrit shanti mantra (peace mantra) that invokes well-being, peace, and prosperity for all. It's often recited during prayers, rituals, and as a closing prayer to bless everyone present, wishing them happiness and harmony.

# HANDS- PALM MANTRA

*Karagre Vasate Lakshmi,*
*Karamadhye Saraswati,*
*Karamoole Tu Govinda,*
*Prabhate Karadarshanam.*

Om, Lakshmi, the Goddess of wealth, resides in the
foremost part of the hands(kara).
Saraswati, the Goddess of learning, resides in the palm.
Govinda, the Lord Narayana resides at the root near the
wrist.
Therefore, every morning, one should have a respectful
look at one's hands.

# SURYANAMASKAR MANTRA

1. *Om Mitraya Namah*
2. *Om Ravaye Namah*
3. *Om Suryaya Namah*
4. *Om Bhanave Namah*
5. *Om Khagaaye Namah*
6. *Om Pushne Namah*
7. *Om Hiranyagarbhaya Namah*
1. *Om Marichye Namah*
2. *Om Aadityaya Namah*
3. *Om Savitre Namah*
4. *Om Arkaaya Namah*
5. *Om Bhaskaraya Namah*

Chants called Sun Salutation Mantras may accompany the Surya Namaskar. These chants bring harmony in body, breath and the mind. As the practice deepens, so do the benefits. When chanted with sincere gratitude, these mantras can take the practice to an enhanced spiritual level.

# PATANJALI YOGA MANTRA

*yogena chittasya padena vacham |*
*malam sharirasya cha vaidyakena ||*
*yo'pakarottamam pravaram muninam |*
*patanjalim pranjaliranato'smi ||*

The mantra "Yogena Chittasya Padena Vacham Malam Sharirasya Ca VaidyaKena Yopa' karottam Pravaram Muninam Patanjalim PranjaliRanato smi" is an invocation to the sage Patanjali, the author of the Yoga Sutras. It means "I praise the most excellent of sages, Patanjali, who gave us Yoga for serenity of mind, grammar for clarity of speech, and medicine for the perfection of health.

# ASHTANGA OPENING MANTRA

*Guru Dhyanam:*
*vande gurūnām caranāravinde sandarśita*
*svātma sukhāvabodhe |*
*nihśreyase jāngalikāyamāne samsāra*
*hālāhala mohaśantyai ||*
*ābāhu purusākāram śankacakrāsi dhārinam |*
*sahasra śirasam śvetam pranamāmi patañjalim ||*

I bow to the lotus feet of the Supreme Guru who reveals
the happiness of Self-Realization, who like the jungle
physician removes the delusion caused by the great poison
of conditioned existence.

**19**

# ASHTANGA CLOSING MANTRA

*Mangala Mantra:*
*oṃ svasti prajābhyaḥ paripālayantām*
*nyāyena mārgeṇa mahīṃ mahīśāḥ .*
*gobrāhmaṇebhya śubhamastu nityam*
*lokā samastā sukhino bhavantu ..*

May the rulers of the earth keep to the path of virtue, for
protecting the welfare of all generations. May the religious,
and all peoples be forever blessed. May all beings everywhere
be happy and free.
Om peace, peace, perfect peace.

# FIVE ELEMENTS MANTRA

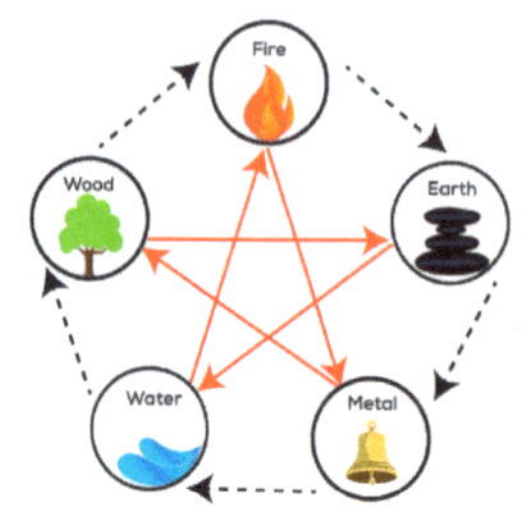


*Om lam pṛthivyai namaḥ*
*Om vam amṛtāya namaḥ*
*Om ram agnaye namaḥ*
*Om yaṁ vāyave namaḥ*
*Om haṁ ākāśāya namaḥ*

*Benefits of Mantras:*
***Balancing:*** *Reciting these mantras can help to balance the corresponding elements within the body and mind.*

***Harmony:*** *Mantras can promote harmony and well-being by aligning with the natural rhythms of the universe.*

***Spiritual Growth:*** *Regular mantra chanting can contribute to spiritual growth and a deeper connection to the self and the cosmos.*

**21**

# IMPORTANCE OF CHAKRAS

Chakras are vital for maintaining physical and mental well-being by regulating energy flow and aligning energetic channels with physical ones. They are believed to be spinning wheels of energy that need to be open and aligned for optimal health. When chakras are balanced, they help regulate body processes, support the immune system, and influence emotions.

# MANTRAS FOR CHAKRAS

### 1. Root Chakra -
*Thumb & index fingers of your hands touch.*
*Sit in the lotus position and place your hands on the knees.*
*Chakra Sound:*
*Long L-A-A-A-M*

### 2. Sacral Chakra -
*Place hands on your laps with your*
*palms facing upwards.*
*Right palm resting on the left.*
*Chakra Sound -*
*Long V-A-A-A-M*

### 3. Solar Plexus Chakra
*Join both of the palms together and place*
*your hands in front of your stomach*
*pointing outwards.*
*Chakra Sound -*
*Long R-A-A-A-M*

### 4. Heart Chakra
*Right hand: Index finger & thumb touching at*
*the heart centre. Left hand in same mudra resting on the knee.*
*Chakra Sound:*
*Long Y-A-A-A-M*

# MANTRAS FOR CHAKRAS

*5. Throat Chakra*
*Hands by stomach, fingers interlaced & thumb*
*tips touching. Focus on the throat area.*
*Chakra Sound:*
*Long H-A-A-A-M*

*6. Third Eye Chakra*

*Hands in front of the lower part of your chest.*
*Middle fingers tips touching, other fingers bent at first joint.*
*Chakra Sound:*
*Long A-A-A-U-U-M*

*7. Crown Chakra*
*Hands in front of your stomach*
*fingers interlaced.*
*Little fingers pointing upwards.*
*Chakra Sound:*
*Long A-A-A-U-U-M*

# BEEJ MANTRAS

*om : Parabrahma, the ultimate reality, sound of creation.*

*śrim : mantra for the Hindu goddess Lakshmi.*
*It is a sacred syllable that represents Lakshmi's divine*
*power and is chanted for wealth, prosperity, and good*
*fortune.*

*aim : This is the bija (seed) mantra of Goddess Saraswati,*
*believed to enhance intellectual abilities and eloquence.*

*gam : associated with Lord Ganesha, the remover of*
*obstacles. It is believed to bring success, victory, and*
*fulfillment of desires.*

*hūm - beej mantra is associated with Lord Shiva and is*
*believed to offer protection from sudden death, fatal*
*diseases, and despair.*

# BEEJ MANTRAS

*klim  : associated with the divine feminine energy, or Shakti. It's believed to attract and enhance relationships, love, and positive connections, effectively manifesting desires and achieving goals.*

*dum : associated with the protective aspect of Goddess Durga. It enhances spiritual strength and protection, providing a shield against negative energies and empowering individuals to overcome obstacles and face challenges with courage and confidence.*

*dam : associated with Lord Vishnu, believed to bring wealth, health, and happiness. It is also said to provide victory, protection from dangers, and a happy married life.*

# GREEN TARA MANTRA

## *Om taare tuttare ture swahah*

The mantra "Om Tare Tuttare Ture Soha" is a powerful invocation for Green Tara, a bodhisattva in Tibetan Buddhism, known for her protective and compassionate nature. The mantra, when translated, broadly means "I take refuge in Tara, the embodiment of all Buddhas' actions, for protection and guidance.

# ABSOLUTE TRUTH MANTRA

*Oṁ asato mā sadgamaya*
*tamasomā jyotir gamaya*
*mrityormāamritam gamaya*
*Oṁ śhānti śhānti śhāntiḥ*

"Asato ma sadgamaya" is a Sanskrit phrase that translates to "Lead us from untruth to truth" or "Lead us from ignorance to knowledge". It's a mantra seeking guidance from a higher power to move from a state of falsehood or misunderstanding to one of enlightenment and understanding.

# HIGHER CONSCIOUSNESS MANTRA

*Om Purnamadah Purnamidam*
*Purnat Purnam Udachyate*
*Purnasya Purnam Adaya*
*Purnam Evavashisyate*
*Om Shanti Shanti Shanti*

Om. That is perfect. This is perfect.
From the perfect springs the perfect.
If the perfect is taken from the perfect, the perfect
remains.
Om. Peace! Peace! Peace!

# MANTRA BEFORE SLEEP

*Om Sarve Bhavantu Sukhinah*
*Sarve Santu Niraamayaah*
*Sarve Bhadraani Pashyantu*
*Maa Kashchid Duhkha Bhaag Bhavet*
*Om Shantih Shantih Shantih*

The "Sarve Bhavantu Sukhinah" mantra is a beautiful and powerful prayer to recite before sleep, promoting peace, well-being, and goodwill for all beings.It's a Shanti Mantra, meaning a peace mantra. The mantra translates to: "May all be happy, may all be free from illness, may all see what is auspicious, may no one suffer.

# END NOTE

As you close the pages of this book, may the mantras you've encountered echo beyond the written word—into your breath, your being, and your daily life.
Each chant is an offering, a vibration of devotion that connects us to the divine source within and around us. In the silence that follows a mantra, there is immense power —a space where healing begins, clarity dawns, and the soul finds its anchor.
This compilation is not the end of your journey, but a companion for it. Return to these mantras in joy, in pain, in stillness, and in motion. Let them become the rhythm of your sādhana, your prayer, your transformation.


With gratitude and reverence,

**Sangeetha Ravindran**
Founder & Director, Sthiti Yoga

www.ingramcontent.com/pod-product-compliance
Lightning Source LLC
Chambersburg PA
CBHW040918110726
48005CB00006B/937